'AFTER THEY PRAYED,
THE PLACE WHERE
THEY WERE MEETING
WAS SHAKEN. AND
THEY WERE ALL FILLED
WITH THE HOLY SPIRIT
AND SPOKE THE WORD
OF GOD BOLDLY.'

// ACTS 4:31

LIVING ON A PRAYER

Welcome to *The Alpha Prayer Guide*. In this simple booklet we describe the practical models of corporate prayer developed at HTB, alongside inspiring testimonies from Alpha Offices and 24-7 Prayer Rooms around the world. We hope it will help you to mobilise people to pray with even greater faith and excitement.

The consistent message from the Bible, from church history and from believers in revival situations is that the key to more power is *more prayer*. It's a message we urgently need to heed in the West today.

At HTB, prayer underpins everything we do from the Alpha Course to the work of the William Wilberforce Trust. Nicky Gumbel describes prayer as: 'the most important activity of our lives.' We therefore offer you these pages in the hope that they may help Alpha churches around the world to experience more of God's presence and power in and through prayer.

C'mon!

Pete Greig
24-7Prayer@Alpha

'THE EVANGELISATION OF THE **WORLD DEPENDS** FIRST UPON A **REVIVAL OF PRAYER.'**

//ROBERT SPEERS

CONTENTS

1. A VISION FOR PRAYER

'I WILL DO WHATEVER YOU ASK IN MY NAME, SO THAT THE FATHER MAY BE GLORIFIED IN THE SON.'

// JOHN 14:13, NLT

'THE NEW TESTAMENT LAYS A **GREATER STRESS ON PRAYER** THAN IT DOES ON THE **EVANGELISATION OF PEOPLE.** THERE IS A **DEEPER NEED** TO PRAY THAN THERE IS EVEN FOR PEOPLE TO BE CONVERTED, AND I DON'T SAY THAT LIGHTLY BECAUSE THERE IS A **FIERCE NEED FOR CONVERSION** BUT CONVERSIONS WON'T HAPPEN **UNLESS** WE ARE PRAYING AND THE BIBLE SAYS THAT FROM BEGINNING TO END.'

// BISHOP SANDY MILLAR

WE HAVE A BIG VISION FOR THE RE-EVANGELISATION OF THE NATIONS AND THE TRANSFORMATION OF SOCIETY. AND THE GOOD NEWS IS THAT GOD HAS PROMISED TO GIVE US PRECISELY THESE THINGS (2 CHRONICLES 7:14). THE BAD NEWS IS THAT THIS PROMISE IS NOT AUTOMATIC; IT IS CONDITIONAL UPON HUMBLE, HOLY AND HUNGRY PRAYER.

'WHEN I SHUT UP THE HEAVENS SO THAT THERE IS NO RAIN, OR COMMAND LOCUSTS TO DEVOUR THE LAND OR SEND A PLAGUE AMONG MY PEOPLE, IF MY PEOPLE, WHO ARE CALLED BY MY NAME, WILL HUMBLE THEMSELVES AND PRAY AND SEEK MY FACE AND TURN FROM THEIR WICKED WAYS, THEN I WILL HEAR FROM HEAVEN, AND I WILL FORGIVE THEIR SIN AND WILL HEAL THEIR LAND.'

// 2 CHRONICLES 7:13–14

The three most important words in this passage may well be the most inconspicuous words too: When ... If ... Then ...

WHEN ... Did you know that God promises us problems? He says 'when', not 'if' trouble comes. As his people we are not immune from the droughts and plagues, which, to an agrarian culture, meant disaster at every level: environmentally, financially and socially.

IF ... Although we are currently experiencing environmental, financial and social crises, as God predicted, so many of his people seem to be placing their hope in products, personalities and programmes instead of doing the one thing God requires: that we turn to him in prayer. There is a big 'If' that acts as a hinge, connecting the prediction of problems ('when') with the most incredible promises of healing and salvation ('then'). We want God to say, 'If problems come, when you pray, then I will act ...' but actually he says the exact opposite: 'When problems come, if you pray, then I will act ...' The enormous challenge facing the West at this time is ultimately not financial, environmental or social but spiritual. Will we, as God's people, turn to him in prayer? The hinge of history has always been the bended knee.

THEN ... When problems come, if we will pray, God promises to make our evangelisation effective ('forgiveness') and to transform society ('healing the land'). In the following section you will read five remarkable testimonies about the power of prayer to change lives, communities and even nations today.

'GOD IS NOT DEAF, BUT LISTENS; MORE THAN THAT, HE ACTS. GOD DOES NOT ACT IN THE SAME WAY, WHETHER WE PRAY OR NOT. PRAYER EXERTS AN INFLUENCE UPON GOD'S ACTIONS, EVEN UPON HIS EXISTENCE.'
// KARL BARTH

2. STORIES OF ANSWERED PRAYER

'YOU WHO ANSWER PRAYER,
TO YOU ALL PEOPLE WILL COME.'
// PSALM 65:2

HOW PRAYER IS CHANGING LIVES ALL AROUND THE WORLD:

2.1 INDIA: HOW PRAYER CHANGES NATIONS; AN INTERVIEW WITH J. VARADARAJ

The Director of Alpha India, J Varadaraj – or simply 'Raj' – is known to thousands as a leader and evangelist. His heart beats with an unusual passion for prayer and in this remarkable interview, Raj shares hard-won insights and precious keys to the kinds of prayer that change nations.

RAJ, I'M TOLD THAT YOU GET UP TO PRAY FROM 1 AM MOST DAYS. WHAT ARE THE KEYS TO SUSTAINING SUCH A REMARKABLE PERSONAL PRAYER LIFE? Over the years I have cultivated a discipline of regular praying. My attention span is twenty minutes. So I have organised my prayer times into twenty-minute slots. Usually I take time to collect myself – a re-gathering of the mind and becoming present to his presence. And then when ready, I read Scripture. I do have regular portions that I read systematically and often there is spontaneous reading too, as led by the Spirit. I have found this imperative to my prayer life. Scripture cleanses the mind of all non-God ideas and fills the heart with faith. I also keep a journal during this time. I have moments of rest and waiting on him in the process.

RAJ // DIRECTOR OF ALPHA INDIA

DO YOU ALWAYS PRAY IN THE SAME WAY? In the initial years of being a Christian, I used to pray loudly for long periods of time. Now it is normal to pray loudly when there is a heavy burden, otherwise it is gentle conversation with God, often in silence. Heart-to-heart. I do have prayer times with others – with a small group on a regular basis, with family daily etc, over the phone with a few friends fairly regularly.

IS PRAYER SOMETHING THAT YOU HAVE ALWAYS FOUND EASY TO DO? Not always. Sometimes it's a struggle. At other times it is easier.

PRAYER IS AN OUT-FLOW AND AN OVERFLOW OF A RELATIONSHIP WITH GOD.

Being rightly related to God and others helps.

WHAT ADVICE WOULD YOU GIVE TO A NEW CHRISTIAN WHO IS STRUGGLING TO PRAY OR IS WONDERING HOW TO PRAY? Keep praying, whether you feel like it or not. Prayer is a spiritual discipline, an acquired habit. Till one acquires it, it might appear tough.

YOU WERE MENTORED BY HENRI NOUWEN (AUTHOR OF *THE WOUNDED HEALER*). WHAT DID HE TEACH YOU ABOUT PRAYER? Three things: To be myself in the presence of God, to wait without hurry and to ask with honesty.

WHY DO WE NEED TO PRAY – CAN'T GOD JUST DO IT ANYWAY? As our Lord taught us in Matthew 6, the Father in heaven knows all our needs before we ask them … So it's a good question: 'Why pray?' One answer is simply that the Father desires to hear his children's voices. He desires to know what is troubling us and how he can make us happy. How he longs to know that our desires are in tune with his. When he knows that we want to fulfil his calling upon us, he will answer.

HOW DO YOU SEE PRAYER CHANGING LIVES IN INDIA?

HISTORICALLY, IN INDIA, PRAYER HAS BEEN THE BACKBONE OF ALL REVIVAL MOVEMENTS.

In the early twentieth century, John Hyde (affectionately known as 'Praying Hyde') prayed continuously for a revival and, during the same period, there were 54,000 baptisms in Punjab area alone. Later on Bakht Sing, a man of prayer, planted hundreds of churches all over the country and the 'Friend's Missionary Prayer Bands' planted several thousand churches. When people seek to pray, their hearts are softened and become more open to the work of the Spirit, allowing transformations to take place.

WHAT IMPACT HAS PRAYER HAD ON ALPHA INDIA AND ITS GROWTH? Encouraging churches associated with us to prevail in prayer for this work has united us spiritually and they have made it their work. We circulate prayer lists regularly to prayer partners. We have found that this corporate prayer brings a sense of awareness that God is in control of his work, a sense of dependency on the author of the work, a sense of confidence that God is with us (and we are not alone) and openness to new relationships and opportunities. The results we see here are answers to many prayers for souls from multitudes in this country.

OVER 400,000 PEOPLE HAVE ATTENDED THE ALPHA COURSE IN INDIA. 11,333 COURSES HAVE TAKEN PLACE AND 158,662 OF THE PEOPLE WHO HAVE BEEN SAVED HAVE JOINED CHURCHES.
// ALPHA INDIA NEWS, ISSUE 1, JANUARY – MARCH 2011

AS SOMEONE PASSIONATE ABOUT PRAYER, WHO ALSO HEADS UP ALPHA INDIA, HOW DO YOU SEE PRAYER AND MISSION FITTING TOGETHER? Mission is the fuel that propels the prayer. One cannot pray much without substance, for prayer is substance in relationship with the Father. It is sharing God's missional heart through our passion for the lost.

WHAT ADVICE WOULD YOU GIVE TO A CHURCH LEADER WHO IS TRYING TO ENCOURAGE HIS CONGREGATION TO PRAY? The life of a church leader is prophetic to the congregation. Prayer life needs to be modelled to the congregation. They need to know when the leader prays. The leader can mentor the congregation to pray by praying with individuals and families. He can show methods of prayer by teaching the congregation. Calling them to pray together periodically, he can mobilise them as a body.

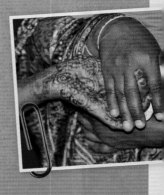

2.2 SOUTH AFRICA: HOW PRAYER CHANGES TOWNSHIPS

BISHOP PETER SEKHONYANE

Bishop Peter Sekhonyane was discouraged. In twenty years as a crusade evangelist he'd led thousands of people to the Lord, yet so few had continued in faith and been integrated into the church. Not knowing anything about the Alpha Course model, he was dejectedly preparing to quit preaching and return to his previous job as a concrete engineer. But then God spoke to him: 'Peter, you evangelised the people but you didn't teach them to pray. Therefore they are not strong enough when trouble and temptation comes. Go now, and teach my people to pray'.

In obedience to this gentle rebuke, Peter erected a 300-seater tent and began training people how to pray in one of the 'extensions' of Orange Farm, a poor township near Cape Town. People flocked to the 24-7 Prayer Tent, interceding night and day for their families and the community. What was even more remarkable was that many of those who came to pray hadn't previously considered themselves Christians.

The idea of 24-7 Prayer quickly caught on and word spread into other areas of the township. Within nine months, Peter had established similar 24-7 Prayer Tents in seven of the twenty extensions. And then came the next great shock:

WHEREVER 24-7 PRAYER WAS ESTABLISHED, THE CRIME RATES BEGAN TO COME DOWN.

In fact the improvement was so dramatic that the police specifically asked Peter to take his prayer tent to a particular village where crime and violence were rampant and they didn't know what to do. After just two weeks of 24-7 Prayer in this new location, crime had declined there too, and before long the police were asking Peter to establish prayer tents in all their worst crime areas.

'Now even the white churches are opening their doors to adopt 24-7 Prayer', says Bishop Peter with a wry smile. 'In fact, the churches that were most involved with apartheid are now the suppliers of the tents we use.'

After five years of 24-7 Prayer in townships across South Africa, Bishop Peter's team carefully analysed their records and calculated the social and spiritual impact of their endeavours. The results are stunning:

- 38 debts cancelled
- 82 misplaced people reconnected
- 190 successful corruption prosecutions
- 2,807 marriages restored
- 7,240 churches have adopted 24-7 Prayer
- 8,400 new businesses established
- 785,300 salvations

Marriages restored. Businesses established. Hundreds of thousands coming to Christ! So many of our greatest passions are reflected in this list, and the key to it all has been persistent prayer.

'AND WILL NOT GOD BRING ABOUT JUSTICE FOR HIS CHOSEN ONES, WHO CRY OUT TO HIM DAY AND NIGHT?' // LUKE 18:7

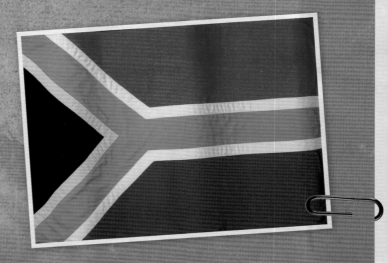

REVD JOHN DICKINSON

2.3 NORTHERN IRELAND: HOW PRAYER CHANGES CHURCHES

Several years ago, we set up a 24-7 Prayer Room for Lent in which we prayed for twenty-four hours every weekend from 10am on a Saturday 'till 10am on a Sunday, and then for the whole of Holy Week finishing just before our Good Friday Service. The people who set up the prayer room and a large proportion of those who took slots during that time had come to faith in Jesus through Alpha. We calculated that more than 140 people prayed at least once in the 24-7 Prayer Room – the biggest prayer meeting we ever had.

When we called a meeting to review our season of 24-7 Prayer and to decide what we had learnt from the experience, everyone said that we should never have stopped it! So a few weeks later we started praying again from 10am on Saturday to 10am on Sunday and, with only a few short breaks,

WE HAVE BEEN PRAYING EVERY WEEKEND EVER SINCE, EXPANDING IT TO FORTY-EIGHT HOURS ON THE WEEKEND BEFORE OUR ALPHA COURSES AND PRAYING 24-7 ALL THROUGH HOLY WEEK.

What all this has done is to drive the development of the prayer life of the congregation by keeping prayer to the forefront constantly. // **REVD JOHN DICKINSON – CARNMONEY PRESBYTERIAN CHURCH, NORTHERN IRELAND**

2.4 SCOTLAND: HOW PRAYER CHANGES ALPHA

A group of St Andrews students recently set up a 24-7 Prayer Room at Holy Trinity Church. They followed this with an Alpha launch party at the Old Course Hotel. Many came to faith as a result. David Simpson, Evangelism Secretary for the CU and Student Alpha Adviser, said, 'I loved seeing Christians fall in love with Jesus in the prayer room and then come out really fired up in their love for him and ready to serve on the missions week. Prayer gives power to our proclamation.'

However, it wasn't even just Christians who were impacted. David's friend Alex was a non-Christian, until he decided to go along to some of the CU missions events and then he ended up in the prayer room. David said, 'Going into the prayer room was a defining moment for Alex, his whole perspective on life changed. He said that he realised that Christians weren't crazies. He said, "They're not just wacky people, but they have stumbled across the most amazing news ever." He went from not being a Christian to encountering God in a very real way and hearing angels sing in church.'

AS A RESULT OF THE PRAYER ROOM, STUDENT ALPHA IN ST ANDREWS HAS BEEN DRAMATICALLY CHANGED.

The students said that Alpha feels different now and the Christians are even more united. They held a launch party with 120 guests at the famous Old Course Hotel and called it 'Alpha Course at the Old Course'. The CU President spoke at that and gave an invitation, 'If Christ is real, why not explore the meaning of life on the Alpha Course?' David said,

ST ANDREWS, THE HOME OF GOLF

'GOD REALLY CAME THROUGH FOR US, EVEN OUR SECURITY GUARDS WERE CHRISTIANS FROM NIGERIA WHO PRAYED FOR US ALL EVENING!

We had a ceilidh as well and we got great feedback from the non-Christians who came. One of them said that he realised now that Christians know how to party!' Lots of international students went as guests and enjoyed a real sense of occasion as well as listening to the talk. Another student involved was Hannah McVeigh. She said, 'I think the guests were definitely surprised by how much fun they had, people don't usually expect Christian events to be fun, but it really was.'

Nick Guy was also instrumental in 24-7 and Alpha. He said that Alpha and the prayer room worked so well together: 'Everyone has their own way of exploring God: some like to be completely quiet, they can go to the prayer room and experience God's presence and see other people loving God. Then other people want the opportunity to ask questions and get answers, Alpha is perfect for them. The two together are very powerful,' he added.

They ran the course in a pub in the centre of town. Hannah McVeigh commented on the impact made, 'My friend, who is not a Christian, had gone out with some mates and at the end of the night they decided to go to the prayer room and check it out. I loved that she felt so free to just pop in. She had a ball, she had never really thought about faith and so enjoyed having a really quiet place to sit and think things through. I am excited to see what happens with her. A lot of people have perceptions about Christianity and I think what is happening in St Andrews is that God is bringing church and faith outside of the box it has been put in, through 24-7 Prayer and Alpha, people can see it's not just about church but that it is about our whole lives.'

NICK GUY

2.5 ENGLAND: HOW PRAYER CHANGES LIVES

This testimony from the first 24–7 Prayer Room in Chichester, England illustrates the power of prayer to impact new Christians.

'LAST NIGHT SOMEONE PRAYED FOR ME AND FOR THE FIRST TIME IN MY LIFE I REALLY FELT GOD ENTER INTO ME AND IT WAS AN INCREDIBLE FEELING (ALMOST LIKE I WAS A CHILD AGAIN) ... AND THEN GOD ACTUALLY TALKED TO ME (SOMETHING I DIDN'T THINK COULD EVER HAPPEN). HIS EXACT WORDS WERE, 'YOU ARE MY SON, I WILL NEVER LEAVE YOU.' HE SAID IT OVER AND OVER AGAIN AND I COULD HEAR MUSIC. I LITERALLY WANTED TO SHOUT OUT TO JESUS. THIS IS THE MOST AMAZING TIME OF MY LIFE AND I WANT EVERYONE TO KNOW. I WANT ALL MY FRIENDS AND THE PEOPLE I WORK WITH TO KNOW.'

SETTING UP THE 24-7 PRAYER ROOM IN CHICHESTER, ENGLAND

2.6 USA: HOW PRAYER CHANGED A CAMPUS

A testimony from a 24-7 Prayer Room in Ohio, USA:
'I was hanging out with my friend Aimee when she told me a very strange thing. She said that she had to leave for an "appointment with God". Something inside me was curious, so when she invited me to come along to the prayer room, I did. During our hour, I accepted Christ and I cannot tell you how life-changing the experience has been for me.

Since that day, I have returned to the 24-7 Prayer Room a few times and God has truly shown himself to me in huge and marvelous ways. You see, I am a kid who grew up with an abusive dad and I believed that I could therefore never experience the love of a father. But God has shown me differently. I have felt so loved and now experience peace everyday knowing that my heavenly Father is with me. I didn't ever think this was something I could feel.

During one of my visits to the prayer room, I saw a card on the wall asking people to pray "for the lost". It was humbling to me to read that because I realized that people I didn't know had been praying for me when I was lost.

I live in a fraternity house at Bluffton University, Ohio, and I couldn't get my frat brothers off my mind. Aimee explained that now that I was a Christian I had been called to seek others out and tell them of the great love I am experiencing. So she prayed that I would have boldness and courage to do this at school.

I began to pray that all thirty-three of my frat brothers would give their lives to Christ. And one by one, they did! It was a little bit crazy. Every couple of days another guy would come and ask me to pray with him or tell me that he had already prayed. How exciting it was for me to watch the transformation in my fraternity house. It had been a place dedicated to anything that didn't honor God, but now we were singing worship songs in our living room!

GOD TOOK OVER OUR HOUSE AND THERE WAS NO TURNING BACK.

By the time we left for Christmas break everyone except Tim had become a Christian.

During break, Aimee was house-sitting and invited Tim over for dinner. By the end of the night he too had placed his faith in Christ as his Savior. Thirty-four frat brothers in less than six months. What a mighty God!

Little did we know how perfect God's timing was in all of this. Twenty-seven days after Tim placed his faith in Christ, just after Christmas, he was involved in a fatal automobile accident and went to be with Jesus.

In the twenty-seven days before Tim died, he had been consumed with concern for his parents who did not yet share his newfound Christian faith. But

AT HIS FUNERAL, TIM'S PARENTS AND FIFTEEN OF HIS HIGH SCHOOL FOOTBALL TEAM-MATES DECIDED TO TRUST CHRIST AND FOLLOW HIM.

I believe all of this happened because there were people in the 24-7 Prayer Room praying for the lost. I praise God for the church and their faithful obedience to God demonstrated through prayer.'

'OF ALL
THINGS,
GUARD
AGAINST
NEGLECTING
GOD IN THE
SECRET
PLACE OF
PRAYER.'

**// WILLIAM
WILBERFORCE**

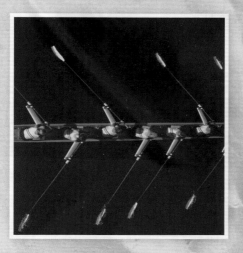

3. MODELS OF
CORPORATE PRAYER

'HOW GOOD AND PLEASANT IT IS WHEN
GOD'S PEOPLE LIVE TOGETHER IN UNITY!'
// **PSALM 133:1**

'THE [PERSON] WHO MOBILIZES THE CHRISTIAN CHURCH TO PRAY WILL MAKE THE GREATEST CONTRIBUTION TO WORLD EVANGELIZATION IN HISTORY.' // ANDREW MURRAY

There are so many new and exciting ways in which people are joining together in prayer for the world and so our hope is that, by sharing the models of prayer we use at HTB, we will equip you to:

- Become more effective in prayer
- Become more strategic in coordinating the corporate prayer life of your church
- Get every member of your church excited about and actively engaged in the priestly mission of the church

IN THIS SECTION WE WILL DESCRIBE ELEVEN PRACTICAL MODELS OF CORPORATE PRAYER, WHICH CAN BE REPRODUCED IN CHURCHES OF ANY SIZE:

3.1 HOW TO RUN REALLY GREAT PRAYER MEETINGS

> 'AGAIN I TELL YOU THAT IF TWO OF YOU ON EARTH AGREE ABOUT ANYTHING YOU ASK FOR, IT WILL BE DONE FOR YOU BY MY FATHER IN HEAVEN. FOR WHERE TWO OR THREE COME TOGETHER IN MY NAME, THERE I AM WITH THEM.' // MATTHEW 18:19

The first Christians knew that prayer meetings are exciting and we don't think anything has changed! On one occasion, the room in which they were meeting shook with the power of their prayers. On another occasion, Peter was miraculously rescued from prison by their prayers. Jesus had told them that when they came together in his name, he would attend, and that when they agreed together in his name, he would hear their prayers and perform miracles. No wonder the instinct of the early church, whenever they faced trials, was simply to raise their voices together in prayer.

Our weekly prayer meeting at HTB runs from 7–8am on a Tuesday morning in the church building. It is the basic building block of our corporate prayer life as a church. The number one aim in leading these prayer meetings is to make sure that they are never ever boring! We do this in four ways:

1. By breaking the hour down into short 'bite-size' sections

2. By deploying different models and styles of prayer throughout

3. By focusing on different issues: personal, local, national, global

4. By blending worship and space for prophetic input in with the prayers too

SIX MODELS OF CORPORATE PRAYER:

1. **ABC:** A great way to actively engage everyone in a prayer meeting is to sometimes split the group into threes, asking each person to allocate themselves 'A', 'B' or 'C'. Having done this, give three specific prayer pointers each relating to a particular issue, allocating one request for A's, one for B's and one for C's. This multiplies the prayer and engages everyone. Each person at the prayer meeting then knows what they are praying about and instead of just one big prayer meeting you end up with lots of smaller groups all praying at once.

2. **Worship:** Of course many of our prayers can be sung, and we are told to bring our petitions before the Lord with thanksgiving and to enter his courts with praise. Therefore, during the prayer meeting try to ebb and flow between sung worship times and intercession, with music playing in the background throughout.

3. **Crying out:** Jesus sometimes prayed 'in a loud voice' and we are told that the early church also 'raised their voices together in prayer to God'. Today, wherever the church is growing fastest it models simultaneous corporate prayer. So even if it feels uncomfortable or unnatural at first, we undoubtedly have something to learn about raising our voices in prayer from Jesus, from the early church and from our brothers and sisters today in places such as South Korea, Indonesia, Nigeria, China and Argentina.

Praying simultaneously is much more efficient since we believe that God can hear each one of us, and it's more engaging than listening passively to long speeches from others until we eventually say 'Amen' at the end. Praying aloud together is also a great way of stirring ourselves to get passionate about things that really matter. You will find it helpful to play music in the background when you pray in this way and it can be important to prime people and to give them a clear prayer focus – something really inspiring.

We will also often encourage people to think of a particular biblical promise to claim if they are not sure what else to say. And the moment that voices start to die down, (I'm afraid that for us this is often after merely a minute or two) be ready to move on to the next thing or flow into a worship song.

4. **50/50:** Another way to engage everyone in prayer (and to make the 'crying out' model a little easier) is to split the group in half, asking one side to raise their voices and cry out to God about a particular issue whilst the other half of the room sings in worship. Then, after a verse or a chorus, swap sides. This is a good way of combining thanksgiving with intercession.

5. **Zones:** You could also split the room into zones and focus the prayers in each section on a different topic or aspect of a single theme. This might simply involve making three or four posters with particular prayer points on each one, and sticking these up on different pillars or walls of the building. Allow enough time for people to move around the room praying silently or quietly into whichever of the issues they choose. It's a good idea to have instrumental music playing softly in the background to make the silence less intimidating. Every few minutes you may like to encourage people to move on to the next zone.

PRAYER MEETING AT HTB

6. **Petitioning the King:** This model of prayer involves placing a chair at the front of the room with its back towards the crowd. Having done this, remind people of the seriousness of prayer and the honour of coming into the presence of a Holy King with our requests. You may like to provide some historical context by mentioning the biblical story of Esther who was afraid that she might be struck dead if her request displeased King Xerxes.

Next, simply ask people to imagine that the chair is a throne and that God is lovingly and graciously inviting them to request of him just one specific thing. What would that supreme request be? Then play music and make space for people to come, one at a time, to kneel before Christ's throne and make their petition reverently to the King. This can be very powerful and emotional as long as it isn't done too often.

27

TIME (MINUTES)	TYPE OF PRAYER	THEME
5	Worship	Adoration
5	Bible focus	The power of prayer: raise faith by sharing recent answers to prayer
5	ABC	Pray for three local church issues
15 minutes		
2	–	Interview/video focus on particular issue (eg, an event in the news)
2	Crying out	Claim God's promises for the situation described
1	–	Introduce next prayer focus (eg, forthcoming Alpha Course)
5	Zones	Each zone focuses on a different challenge: guests / speakers / logistics, etc
2	Petition	Allow people to bring their biggest heart cry before God
1	–	Introduce next theme (eg, problems with youth group)
2	50/50	50 % pray for teenagers / 50 % prayer for their parents
15 minutes		
7	Worship	Choose petitioning lyrics if possible
5	Listen	Space for sharing prophetic encouragements
3	ABC	Pray into issues raised by words of knowledge
15 minutes		
1	–	Introduce next prayer focus (eg, mission)
5	ABC	Pray by name for three missionaries associated with your church
7	Worship	Thanksgiving
2	-	Closing prayer and notices
15 minutes		
[light breakfast served]		

'I ATTEND THE HTB PRAYER MEETING BECAUSE I BELIEVE THAT WHEN WE PRAY GOD HEARS US IN HEAVEN AND THINGS HAPPEN. THINGS CHANGE BECAUSE WE GET UP, GET TOGETHER AND PRAY. IT'S THE HIGHLIGHT OF MY WEEK'. // THE REVD BILL CAHUSAC

3.2 SOCIAL JUSTICE PRAYER BRIEFINGS

It was a normal church prayer meeting at our annual 'Focus' church holiday. A friend, who had recently set up a charity to fight human trafficking in India, happened to be present and so we asked him to come and say a few words so that we could support his endeavour with five minutes of prayer. He's a successful businessman; a very competent and 'together' sort of person, but

WHEN HE TRIED TO SPEAK HE SIMPLY BROKE DOWN IN TEARS.

He couldn't say a word. He just wept. And as he did so, a great seriousness entered the room. It was as though we caught something of God's heart for the children who are crying out to him for help. We realised then and there that we simply had to start praying regularly for the things that break God's heart. We had to put our prayers where our preaching is.

The prophet Isaiah insists that we must not separate our prayer lives from the lives of those who are hurting and oppressed (Isaiah 58). The apostle Paul reminds us that 'Our battle is not against flesh and blood but against principalities and powers in high places' (Ephesians 6:18). As well as engaging with major world issues practically, we believe that God's people must wrestle with them prayerfully.

To do this we produce a monthly 'prayer briefing' which focuses the intercessions of the church on a particular social justice issue such as human trafficking, the AIDS crisis, the persecuted church, caring for the environment, broken families at Christmas and peace in the Middle East.

Each briefing is included in the monthly church information guide so that everyone who attends a service hears about it. The briefing combines relevant scriptures, key facts supplied by experts in the field and specific prayer pointers. As well as encouraging church members to pray throughout the month about this particular social justice issue, we also devote one of our weekly prayer meetings to the theme and invite a knowledgeable person to come and help inform our prayers. One of the exciting implications of doing this is that people who might not normally attend the prayer meeting may well be galvanised to attend when we are addressing an issue about which they care passionately.

STEPS FOR CREATING A PRAYER BRIEFING:

1. **Choose the topic:** Are people in your church passionate about any particular issues? Are there any national campaigns you could support in prayer? Are there local issues of injustice in your community or city that need to be addressed? These could be anything from gun-crime on the streets to the closing down of neighbourhood schools.

2. **Research the issue:** It's important that the briefing wins hearts and minds in order to motivate prayer. Therefore take time to research and find powerful statistics and moving stories to inform and inspire prayer.

3. **Prepare the briefing and prayer points:** Collate and summarise everything you have researched into a few bullet points and verses with perhaps one short story. It's important not to overwhelm people with information. Seven prayer points, one for every day of the week, is ideal. Keep it simple and compelling. Disseminate this information through church news-sheets, website, Facebook, emails to your prayer network (see section 3.3) or create a special leaflet that can be handed out on Sundays for attachment to fridges, notice boards or insertion in Bibles.

JUSTICE AND CARE

4. **Invite a guest:** If you know of a non-profit organisation linked to the topic you are praying about, see if there is someone who might come and offer a ten-minute interview as part of your prayer meeting. Alternatively, you may have someone in your community who is already knowledgeable and compelling on the subject.

5. **Publicise your prayer meeting:** Encourage your congregation that if they care about the issue and want to make a difference they really can do so by coming to the special prayer meeting.

To see an example of an HTB prayer briefing go to htb.org.uk/prayerbriefing

'WE ARE CONVINCED IT WAS THAT MORNING PRAYING [ABOUT HUMAN TRAFFICKING] AT HTB, A COUPLE OF WEEKS AGO THAT HAS CAUSED THE TIDE TO TURN IN OUR FAVOUR. SO MUCH SO, IN THE LAST RAID, THE ADDITIONAL COMMISSIONER OF POLICE SENT IN HIS OWN SPECIAL FORCE TEAM WITH THE RAID.'

// ASHLEY VARGHESE, JUSTICE & CARE INTERNATIONAL

3.3 PRAYER NETWORKS

A child is suddenly struck down on the way to school and she is lying in a critical condition in hospital. A new Christian is struggling with his faith. Members of a Global Alpha Training (GAT) team have all contracted food poisoning. Sunday's preacher has lost his voice.

Some prayer requests just can't wait for the weekly prayer meeting. Others are too confidential for public broadcast. And anyway, whenever and wherever you hold the church prayer meeting, it will always be an impossible time or place for some church members to attend, no matter how much they may want to pray.

It's so exciting, therefore, that we live in a time when it is possible to connect and communicate instantly and affordably at the touch of a few buttons, and we can use this to mobilise prayer.

When we surveyed the HTB congregations three years ago, we discovered that many people wanted to grow in prayer and were keen to be given prayer requests too. What was particularly interesting was the discovery that the number of people expressing a hunger for prayer was more than four times higher than the number attending the weekly prayer meeting.

So we launched a prayer network called **PrayerForce**, which identifies those church members with a heart for prayer and sends them regular confidential prayer alerts via email, text, Facebook or a password protected website. In return we try to help them grow in their own prayer lives by arranging occasional quiet day retreats, providing relevant teaching and by sending out a newsletter, which includes quotes, testimonies of answered prayer, and extracts from helpful books.

One of the great things about the PrayerForce model is that it can work in a very small church where there might be just three people with a heart for prayer, or in a large church where there may be many hundreds.

'AN EXCITING PART OF PRAYERFORCE IS GETTING THE EMAILS AND KNOWING THAT I MAKE A DIFFERENCE BY PRAYING INDIVIDUALLY. I'M A STUDENT AND I DON'T HAVE THE TIME TO ATTEND EVERYTHING AT HTB, SO PRAYERFORCE IS ONE WAY THAT I MAKE A DIFFERENCE' // PRAYERFORCE MEMBER

3.4 24-7 PRAYER ROOMS

24-7 Prayer is one of the most exciting and creative expressions of prayer in churches around the world, including HTB. We arrange regular seasons of 24-7 (night-and-day) prayer in a specially decorated room on site. People can sign up to take an hour-long shift in the prayer room, and we thereby fill days and even weeks with non-stop intercession and praise as part of the global 24-7 Prayer movement. This has been going for more than a decade in multiple locations continually.

We are planning to expand our 24-7 Prayer seasons at HTB to start praying continually throughout the year. Since Alpha ministries operate all over the world, it makes perfect sense to have a prayer room that is functioning at the heart of everything, beating night-and-day, in which we can respond to prayer requests from any time zone on earth, whenever they come in.

33

'IN ALBANIA, WHEN WE STARTED THE FIRST 24-7 PRAYER ROOM, IT COINCIDED WITH THE START OF ALPHA AND THE START OF OUR TRAINING CENTRE FOR LEADERSHIP AND BOTH MINISTRIES ARE VERY SUCCESSFUL. WE CREDIT IT ALL REALLY TO THE 24-7 PRAYER ROOM.' // **HERVIN FUSHIATI, ALBANIA**

WHAT IS 24-7 PRAYER?

The 24-7 Prayer model is a simple idea. It's just praying without stopping, in one-hour shifts, night-and-day, around the clock, in a room or space that's been set aside as a 'prayer room'. Groups tend to pray like this for anything from twenty-four hours up to many months. The room is decorated creatively to inspire prayer, engaging as many of the senses as possible, and enabling people to experiment with different styles and types of prayer.

A season of 24-7 Prayer provides a place, a time, a context and a catalyst for prayer. It's a practical tool helping ordinary people to pray. Many who would consider themselves bad at praying turn up for their hour slot in the prayer room and then stay for two. One is rarely enough.

The 24-7 model of night and day prayer has been field-tested extensively since 1999 in many nations, most denominations and locations as diverse as English cathedrals, a van in the slums of Delhi and a brewery in Missouri. It's especially exciting when 24-7 Prayer leads up to an Alpha Course or even runs concurrently.

HTB'S 24-7 PRAYER ROOM

COUNTLESS PEOPLE HAVE EMERGED FROM PRAYER ROOMS TO REPORT THAT GOD SPOKE TO THEM IN LIFE CHANGING WAYS, or that they found prayer easier, or that an hour felt like ten minutes. Even non-Christians have often experienced God's presence.

WHERE DID THE IDEA COME FROM?

Church history reveals that 24-7 Prayer vigils have always been used powerfully by God:

- **2000 years ago:** The church was born in a 24-7 Prayer Room in Jerusalem!
- **1000 years ago:** Celtic monasteries prayed 24-7 and transformed Europe
- **300 years ago:** Moravians prayed 24-7 for 100 years and took the gospel to many nations
- **105 years ago:** A multi racial 24-7 Prayer Room on Azusa street in Los Angeles sparked the global Pentecostal and Charismatic renewal

Such historical precedents make it even more exciting that a new generation is discovering the power of 24-7 Prayer, especially when it is twinned with Alpha.

To find out more about 24-7 Prayer and how to set up a prayer room:

- visit 24-7Prayer.com
- *The 24-7 Prayer Manual* explains how to organise a season of non-stop prayer
- *Red Moon Rising* tells the exciting story of how the 24-7 Prayer movement began

'I HAVE TO ADMIT WHEN YOU SUGGESTED I GO TO THE PRAYER ROOM I DID IT MORE OUT OF A SENSE THAT YOU HAD SUGGESTED IT THAN ANYTHING ELSE, BUT IT WAS AMAZING! I CAN'T REALLY EXPLAIN IT, BUT WHEN I ARRIVED I WASN'T REALLY SURE WHAT TO DO, SO I STARTED PRAYING FOR THE WORLD AND THEN GOD JUST SHOWED UP. IT TOOK ME TOTALLY BY SURPRISE. NOT JUST THAT, BUT THE MORE I PRAYED, THE MORE I SEEMED TO WANT TO PRAY FOR OTHERS.'

3.5 PRAYER CONCERTS

One of the most exciting ways of praying can be to arrange a prayer concert, combining worship with prayer, space to be still and listen to God, and also gaps when people can share their own testimonies and impressions with the group.

The Psalms are an extraordinary combination of adoration, thanksgiving, lamentation, petition and intercession, written mostly for corporate singing and recitation. The divide between 'worship' and 'prayer' is often a false one – they are really two sides of the same coin. After all, the apostle Paul advises us to bring our petitions before the Lord with thanksgiving.

To make prayer concerts really flow, it's important that the worship leader and the prayer leader work closely together and are flexible, open to the leading of the Spirit. Speaking should be kept to a minimum – this is not a mini church service and no one wants a sermon! Other than a short introduction at the beginning to help focus faith, try to keep talk, rules and liturgy to a minimum. You will find a natural flow emerges between worship and prayer, thanksgiving and petition, noise and silence.

PRAYER & WORSHIP CONCERT AT FOCUS, HTB'S ANNUAL HOLIDAY

PRAYER AND FASTING

Twice a year (between our biannual 'Vision Sunday' and 'Gift Sunday') we call the church to a day of prayer and fasting. It is a way of coming together as a community to focus our prayers on the vision and ministries God has given us. The day begins with our regular Tuesday prayer meeting from 7–8am and concludes twelve hours later, from 7–8pm with a prayer concert led by Tim Hughes and Pete Greig. After this event, everyone is encouraged to go and break their fast in groups, perhaps in one of the nearby restaurants.

Fasting humbles us and brings us to an awareness of our need of God. It renews the sense of balance and priority in our walk with God. It heightens our spiritual sensitivity and clears the channels of communication with God. It hits at our deep-seated selfishness and strengthens our self control. Having a dedicated time of prayer and fasting is not a way of manipulating God into doing what you desire. Rather, it is simply forcing yourself to focus and rely on God for the strength, provision, and wisdom you need.

SPECIAL OCCASIONS

Every year at HTB we also hold a New Year Prayer Concert, which offers the congregation an alternative to the usual New Years Eve parties. It's an opportunity to focus on Jesus, a time to look back on the year that has passed and to pray for the year ahead. We celebrate with great worship, lots of fun, prayers, moments of quiet reflection and a satellite link-up to Big Ben at midnight.

We encourage churches to hold special prayer events as part of the annual Alpha Invitation campaign (see section 4).

3.6 YEARS OF PRAYER

Why not join other churches from around your country in taking part in a Year of Prayer? One people, joined together in constant prayer for the evangelisation of your nation and the transformation of society. This exciting model of joined-up, national-local intercession has been growing in many different contexts over recent years:

- Scottish Alpha churches combined with others in a year of unbroken 24-7 Prayer throughout 2010. The initiative was known as 'The Big If ...' – a reference to 2 Chronicles 7:14 'If my people ...'
- Alpha USA partnered with 24-7 Prayer to catalyse 'Campus America': a year of missional prayer on hundreds of US campuses
- In 2011, a similar year of united prayer took place throughout Ireland

KC:UK2012 – FOUR NATIONS, ONE YEAR OF 24-7 PRAYER: 'KINGDOM COME'

UK: In 2012 we are inviting all 7000 Alpha churches in the UK to come together for an unbroken year of prayer throughout England, Wales, Scotland and Northern Ireland, filling the Olympic year with unprecedented intercession for the nation. For more information, go to alpha.org/kingdomcome

Global: Also in 2012 we are mobilising prayer globally with each of the fifty Alpha Offices taking responsibility for at least one week of 24-7 Prayer to fill the year with a global chorus of prayer for the Alpha vision. To find out more go to alpha.org/prayer

3.7 THE LORD'S PRAYER AT NOON

The 'Our Father' is the best-known prayer in the world and we are rediscovering its power. On Easter Day alone some two billion people pray or sing these words, first taught by Jesus to the disciples in response to the request, 'Lord, teach us to pray'. In fact, when the Archbishop of Canterbury, Rowan Williams, was asked how he would summarise the entire teaching of Christianity on the back of an envelope he answered without hesitation that he would simply write the words of the Lord's Prayer.

With the growth of the 24-7 Prayer networks around the world, many people have been rediscovering the ancient discipline of pausing each day at noon, in order to pray the 'Our Father'. Christians in so many time zones are now making this a personal discipline that we will soon be a giant global chorus, beginning every hour of every day with the words Christ himself taught us.

Praying the Lord's Prayer at noon is just another tool, alongside the Bible in One Year and a regular visit to a 24-7 Prayer Room, which can help us all to practise the presence of God in our lives twenty-four hours a day and seven days a week. Of course, sometimes when your alarm goes off on your cell phone at noon, it is inconvenient to pause and pray. In many ways that is the whole point; we want our busyness to be rudely and regularly interrupted by a reminder of our deepest priorities in life.

One of the vergers at HTB said that this particular discipline has been the most helpful prayer model he's ever tried because it helps him to remember God in the middle of his working day and to really remember who he is working for.

Of course, such disciplines in prayer do not have to be legalistic 'vain repetition'. In fact they can be liberating and life-giving. As a God-fearing Jew, Jesus would certainly have paused three times every day to pray the Sh'ma: 'Hear, O Israel ...' Such liturgical disciplines have been integral to Christian prayer from the start. For instance, we know that the first believers still attended the daily prayer meetings at the temple. It was on the way to one of these prayer meetings that Peter and John healed the beggar at the gate called Beautiful (Acts 3:1). And in the didache – a letter instructing churches in how to worship, written around the year 100 AD – Christians are encouraged to pray the Lord's Prayer not just once but three times a day (just as Jewish people pray the sh'ma). It's thrilling to think that by praying the Lord's Prayer at noon we are discovering an ancient discipline that connects us with Christians around the world, and back down 2000 years to the very birth of the church.

3.8 PRAYER MINISTRY

'"RAISE UP YOUR STAFF AND STRETCH OUT YOUR HAND OVER THE SEA TO DIVIDE THE WATER SO THAT THE ISRAELITES CAN GO THROUGH THE SEA ON DRY GROUND" THEN MOSES STRETCHED OUT HIS HAND OVER THE SEA ...' // EXODUS 14:16, 21–22

The word 'ministry' is used in several different ways in the New Testament and in the church today. In one sense, ministry includes everything done in a church. John Wimber defined ministry as, 'Meeting the needs of others on the basis of God's resources'. In this section we are focusing just on prayer ministry; when we pray for others in the power of the Holy Spirit.

As the passage above from Exodus explains prayer ministry is cooperation between God and us. This is a ministry for the whole body of Christ, for the whole church – for everybody. Part of Jesus' ministry was praying for people to be healed and set free. When he died and rose again that ministry didn't end. He gave that ministry to his church, his people; he gave it to us. Praying for others is something we can all do.

The model we use for praying for people at HTB follows four simple values:

1. **The ministry of the Holy Spirit:** When we ask the Holy Spirit to come, he comes in power. But at the same time, we need to get the perspective right and keep everything focused on the gospel: Jesus' life, death and resurrection. John 15:5 says, 'I am the vine; you are the branches. If a person remains in me and I in him, he will bear much fruit; apart from me you can do nothing.' When we pray for people it is God who does the work, not us. It's his anointing, his gifts, his power; it all comes from him and it's all because of the cross. Recognising it's the Holy Spirit's ministry and not ours, we aim for simplicity and truthfulness in all aspects when we pray for people.

2. **Biblical authority:** We believe the Spirit of God and the written word of God never conflict. Everything that the Holy Spirit does is, and should be, supported by the Bible. Prayer and the power of the Holy Spirit are not separate from the Scriptures, but integral to them. The Bible tells us, in John 8:32, that the truth will set us free. Therefore we encourage people, when they pray, to build on biblical truths and promises, to ensure that what we are praying for is based on the Bible and not on anything else.

3. **The dignity of the individual:** When we pray for people it is very important that we treat them with respect and dignity. People are often quite nervous when they ask for prayer for the first time, especially if they are from outside the church. It's essential to maintain confidentiality, what you are praying is just between you, them and God. When praying it's important to ensure that you always affirm and encourage the person and don't condemn them. The ultimate goal is that the people we pray for meet with Jesus.

4. **The Body of Christ:** Long-term healing and long-term solutions to people's problems and spiritual growth take place within the church and within the Christian community as a whole. For example, when we pray for people on the Alpha Course we remember that this is just the beginning. Our aim is that guests on Alpha enter into the Christian community once they have completed the course.

I STARTED OUT BY PRAYING IN A 'TAG TEAM' WITH A MORE EXPERIENCED MAN FROM CHURCH (PROBABLY TO PREVENT ME KILLING ANYONE BY MISTAKE). WE PRAYED FOR PEOPLE, BUT I REALLY BELIEVED IT WAS THE OTHER GUY'S PRAYERS THAT COUNTED, NOT MINE. ONE SUNDAY, THERE WERE LOADS OF PEOPLE WANTING PRAYER. THE PERSON LEADING THE MINISTRY SAID, 'MIKE, WE DON'T HAVE ENOUGH PEOPLE TO PRAY, YOU'RE GOING TO HAVE TO PRAY ON YOUR OWN TONIGHT.' I THOUGHT, 'OH NO! I CAN'T PRAY ON MY OWN, I'M NOT SPIRITUAL, I'M NOT HOLY, NOTHING WILL HAPPEN.' I JUST PANICKED AND HOPED THAT THE PERSON I WAS GOING TO PRAY FOR WOULD ONLY HAVE SOMETHING SMALL, LIKE A HEADACHE. THE GUY I WENT UP TO ASKED ME TO PRAY FOR TWO THINGS:

A BAD BACK AND REALLY BAD DEPRESSION. I SAID, 'OKAY, LET'S PRAY FOR THE DEPRESSION FIRST.' (I CHOSE THIS BECAUSE I THOUGHT IT WOULD BE HARDER TO TELL WHETHER OR NOT HE WAS HEALED – THAT WAY HE WOULDN'T NOTICE THAT MY PRAYERS DIDN'T WORK.) I PUT MY HAND ON HIS SHOULDER, AND SAID SOME WORDS. INSIDE I WAS THINKING, 'OH GO ON LORD, PLEASE. JUST THIS ONCE. I'LL DO ANYTHING, EVEN BE NICE TO MY SISTER', BUT OUTSIDE I WAS TRYING TO LOOK VERY SPIRITUAL. I THOUGHT I'D PRAY FOR A SHORT TIME AND THEN EXPLAIN WHY SOMETIMES PEOPLE DON'T GET HEALED.

SUDDENLY, THE GUY OPENED HIS EYES AND SAID, 'THAT'S AMAZING – MY DEPRESSION'S LIFTED, I FEEL LIKE I CAN LAUGH FOR THE FIRST TIME IN AGES!'

I TRIED TO LOOK CONFIDENT, AS IF I'D EXPECTED THAT AND SAID, 'SHALL WE GO FOR THE DOUBLE AND PRAY FOR YOUR BACK TOO?' I PUT MY HAND ON HIS BACK AND PRAYED INSIDE MY HEAD, 'GO ON, GO ON LORD, DO ANOTHER ONE.' AFTER A WHILE, HE OPENED HIS EYES AND SAID, 'THANK YOU FOR PRAYING FOR ME.' I THOUGHT, 'THAT MEANS HIS BACK IS NOT HEALED.' STILL, I WAS PRETTY PLEASED, BECAUSE ONE OUT OF TWO AIN'T BAD!

LATER, I WAS TALKING TO SOMEONE ELSE WHEN THE SAME GUY RAN UP AND SAID, 'LOOK, I'VE JUST REALISED I CAN DO THIS', AND HE STARTED DOING ALL SORTS OF THINGS WITH HIS BODY – HIS BACK WAS HEALED. I LEFT THAT NIGHT WALKING ON AIR.

MIKE PILAVACHI

3.9 PRAYER WALKING

Do you ever feel restricted in prayer meetings? Do you sometimes feel that you should be out amongst the people you are praying for so that you can see the actual streets, businesses and locations where you want the kingdom to come? Then why not take your prayer meeting outside and try prayer walking (or prayer driving)? Prayer walking is intercessory, incarnational prayer on the move! Instead of just praying for a community from the confines of the church it is stepping out into the neighbourhood and making contact with the people and places you are praying for. It's what Jesus did when he left heaven and came to dwell amongst us physically. In their book *Prayer Walking*, Steve Hawthorne and Graham Kendrick describe it as 'praying on-site with insight'. On site we can look, learn and listen to God for real people and places, letting the Holy Spirit guide us as we pray.

'I WILL GIVE YOU EVERY PLACE WHERE YOU SET YOUR FOOT.' // JOSHUA 1:3

GUIDELINES FOR PRAYER WALKING:

- Prayer walking is best done in pairs or groups of three. If there is more than one group of people it is good to have a start and end location and a time when everyone should be back

- As you walk around pray with your eyes open and ask God to show you his heart for the particular place you are walking. Ask him to guide your eyes

- You may like to note down any thoughts or impressions you have

- As you walk, God may speak to you about a particular location, building, or group of people. Ask God to guide your prayers

- When you don't know what to pray, simply speak blessings and pray for the fulfilment of God's promises over the area

- At the end come together and share what God has been saying and how he has guided you

- Even after the walk, continue to pray for the things that God has shown you

TWO AND A HALF YEARS AGO OUR PASTORATE (SMALL GROUP) FELT COMPELLED TO MOVE FROM SOMEBODY'S HOME TO MEET ON THE WORLD'S END ESTATE, A HIGH-RISE COUNCIL ESTATE IN WEST LONDON – AN AREA WITH ABOUT 5,000 PEOPLE, MANY OF WHOM LIVE IN GREAT POVERTY. WE WEREN'T SURE WHY THE LORD WAS DRAWING US THERE, BUT WE WENT THERE IN FAITH. THE FIRST THING WE DID AS A PASTORATE WAS TO TAKE PART IN A PRAYER WALK, SOMETHING WE HAVE DONE REGULARLY EVER SINCE. I REMEMBER THE FIRST PRAYER WALK WHEN I ASKED THE LORD, 'WHAT ARE WE DOING HERE?' IN MY MIND I SAW AN IMAGE OF TALL DARK BUILDINGS WITH A FEW VERY DIM LIGHTS THAT STARTED TO GET BRIGHTER. I ALSO SAW THAT MANY MORE LIGHTS STARTED TO APPEAR AND BECAME BRIGHTER UNTIL I COULD SEE LIGHTS AT ALL LEVELS OF THE BUILDINGS. IT SEEMED AS THOUGH THE LORD WAS SAYING THAT HE IS GOING TO MOVE INTO ALL THE PLACES OF DARKNESS ON THE ESTATE.

ON ANOTHER OCCASION I FELT THE LORD SAY, 'I WILL BRING ALONG SOME MEN WHO BE A BLESSING TO HIS WORK ON THE ESTATE', AND THAT THEY MAY AT FIRST SEEM UNLIKELY BY VIRTUE OF THEIR BACKGROUND, BUT IT IS THEIR BACKGROUNDS THAT WILL INSPIRE OTHERS TO BECOME FOLLOWERS OF JESUS.

TODAY I CAN SEE THAT BOTH OF THESE VISIONS RECEIVED ON PRAYER WALKS ARE BEING REALISED. A GROUP OF TEENAGERS HAS FORMED AND MOST HAVE GIVEN THEIR LIVES TOTALLY TO CHRIST. THEY HAVE CALLED THEMSELVES 'THE CIRCLE' AND REGULARLY MEET IN DIFFERENT HOMES ALL OVER THE ESTATE. VARIOUS OUTREACH PROGRAMMES HAVE BEEN SET UP AND WE KNOW THAT THE LIGHT AND HOPE OF THE LORD IS DRIVING AWAY THE DARKNESS ACROSS THE WHOLE ESTATE. PRAISE THE LORD.

TODAY WE HAVE TWO EX-OFFENDERS IN OUR PASTORATE, BOTH OF WHOM HAVE SPENT LONG PERIODS IN PRISON FOR SOME OF THE BIGGEST DRUG BUSTS IN HISTORY. I CAN THINK OF TWO OTHER AMAZING MEN WHO HAVE ALSO JOINED US, WHO HAVE SUFFERED WITH DEPRESSION IN THE PAST, AND BOTH HAVE HAD THEIR LIVES CHANGED DRAMATICALLY BY THEIR FAITH. TODAY THEY ARE ALL CHANGED MEN AND HAVE VERY POWERFUL TESTIMONIES OF HOW JESUS HAS CHANGED THEIR LIVES AND THEY HAVE GREAT HEARTS FOR PEOPLE ON THE ESTATE.

IT IS AMAZING TO SEE HOW OUR HEAVENLY FATHER HAS MOVED ON THE ESTATE AND IN OUR LIVES IN THE LAST TWO AND A HALF YEARS. I HAVE BECOME A MENTOR TO ONE OF THE EX-OFFENDERS AND THIS HAS CHANGED MY LIFE. I CAN SAY I SEE A LOT MORE OF WHAT THE LORD SEES AS A RESULT OF PRAYER WALKING IN FAITH. WE DID NOT KNOW WHERE THE LORD WAS TAKING US, BUT LOOKING BACK IT HAS BEEN AN EXCITING AND UNFORGETTABLE JOURNEY.

WORLD'S END ESTATE – WEST LONDON

Picture used with permission by Chris Tubb, flicker.com/photos/tubb

'THE WIND BLOWS WHEREVER IT PLEASES. YOU HEAR ITS SOUND, BUT YOU CANNOT TELL WHERE IT COMES FROM OR WHERE IT IS GOING. SO IT IS WITH EVERYONE BORN OF THE SPIRIT.' // JOHN 3:8

revivalrun.org
be the adventure

Like all the best ideas, the Revival Run vision is very simple: Just go wherever God tells you to go and when you arrive plant a simple wooden 'prayer stake' in the ground, and pray your most generous, boldest prayer for the church in that area.

All you have to do is make a load of simple 6 inch 'prayer stakes' out of cheap wood (see www.revivalrun.org for details), and then send one another out to pray a blessing in Jesus' name. This Revival Run vision, which began with a church in Margate, UK in 2011 and has spread all over the world, is simply to scatter blessing, to go on modern day pilgrimages, to be good news to those on the way and to pray for revival in places other than our own. It takes childish faith, hope and courage to act.

Here are some quick tips on how it's done:

- Gather some friends and decide where to go (Jesus always sent people out in two's)
- Make your prayer stake (or have some sent to you through revivalrun.org)
- Set the date and simply ... go and pray
- Take some photos/video and make a story of your Revival Run
- Post it online and share your story

IN JANUARY 2011, GOD TOLD US TO GO AND PRAY FOR REVIVAL IN THE MOST NORTHERLY UK MAINLAND CHURCH (A PLACE CALLED SKARFSKERRY). AS WE DID SO, OUR CHURCH BACK HOME, 760 MILES AWAY, GATHERED TOGETHER, THEN BROKE INTO SMALL TEAMS AND SPENT THE EVENING TRAVELLING TO DIFFERENT PLACES PRAYING BOLD PRAYERS AND PLANTING PRAYER STAKES.

THESE WERE NOT TAME PRAYERS OR RESERVED REQUESTS (HOLDING BACK THE BEST FOR THEMSELVES) BUT THESE PRAYERS WERE WILD, AUDACIOUS AND GENEROUS. PRAYING THAT GOD WOULD GO FAR BEYOND ANY DREAM OR DESIRE THAT THEY MIGHT HAVE FOR THEMSELVES AND ASKING IT FOR ANOTHER PLACE, CHURCH, COLLEGE, BUSINESS AND SUCH LIKE … THE RESULTS HAVE BEEN QUITE SIMPLY AMAZING.

SINCE THAT DAY, THOUSANDS OF PRAYER STAKES HAVE BEEN GIVEN AWAY TO CHURCHES, EVENTS, YOUTH GROUPS AND HUNDREDS OF THOUSANDS OF MILES HAVE BEEN TRAVELLED BY PEOPLE WITH A SIMPLE DESIRE TO GIVE THEIR BEST PRAYERS AWAY FOR ANOTHER.

MIKE ANDREA

3.10 PROPHECY/LISTENING PRAYER

'THOSE WHO SPEAK IN A TONGUE DO NOT SPEAK TO PEOPLE BUT TO GOD. INDEED NO ONE UNDERSTANDS THEM; THEY UTTER MYSTERIES WITH THEIR SPIRITS. BUT THOSE WHO PROPHESY SPEAK TO THE PEOPLE FOR THEIR STRENGTHENING, ENCOURAGEMENT AND COMFORT.' // 1 CORINTHIANS 14:2–3

Prophecy is the heart of God forthtelling (not fortune telling). Much of the Bible is prophetic, it is one of the revelatory gifts (1 Corinthians 12:7–10) and anyone can prophesy (14:31). The Bible tells us to 'Eagerly desire the spiritual gifts, especially the gift of prophecy' (14:1). In the context of prayer, prophecy is the words of God's heart for an individual. The purpose of prophecy is to encourage, strengthen, and comfort (14:3). Its impact on lives is immeasurable. Prophecy has the power to release words of destiny and calling over people's lives and to bring deep comfort to an individual in a difficult situation. It never, ever contradicts the Bible.

We are programmed to hear from God! The prophetic gift flows from our intimate relationship with Jesus. There are different ways of hearing God. Sometimes just an impression, often a scripture, will jump out. We, like Samuel can 'see' pictures and visions from God. Sometimes there will be specific words you feel are from God. Like exercising an under used muscle, this takes practise but will grow stronger with use!

A word of warning – there are barriers to hearing. Our emotions and opinions need to be submitted to God in confession. Always offer words with humility, ask if the word resonates and give people permission to weigh or test the word.

LISTENING PRAYER

Prayer is a two-way conversation. At HTB, the ministry of 'Listening Prayer' seeks to strengthen, encourage and comfort those in our community through sensitive prophetic prayer ministry on an individual level.

Listening Prayer encourages a deeper understanding of repentance, exercising spiritual authority and learning more of our identity in Christ. We have seen many set free from past hurts and injustices, as well as overcoming fear, insecurity and unhealthy behavioural patterns in their lives. Our desire is to truly see people living in the freedom that Christ came to give.

Over a number of evenings pastorate members are invited to spend 30–45 minutes with two or three of our trained Listening Prayer team. A typical appointment includes a time of listening to God, feedback to the guest and then the laying on of hands whilst the team pray into what they have received, where appropriate.

The Listening Prayer team will have completed a practical six-week course in advance of joining the team. Currently, we follow the *Living Free Course Manual*, written by Mike Riches of The Sycamore Commission, and then spend time in further sessions exploring the ways of listening and hearing from God.

The topics covered in the course are:

- Created with a Purpose
- Recovering God's Freedom
- One World, Two Realms
- Understanding Power and Authority
- Strongholds
- Generational Sins, Soul-Ties, and Curses

TRIAL PROPHETIC EXERCISE

This simple exercise can be practiced in a group or on your own. Before beginning, pray, asking the Lord to help you clear your mind and heart and that he would speak to you.

1. Where is Jesus in the room?
2. What is Jesus doing? Look for more detail.
3. What is Jesus wearing?
4. Ask Jesus why he is there?
5. Ask Jesus how you can co-operate with what he is doing?

Do this often and begin to see into the spiritual realm.

- Ask the Holy Spirit about people – press in asking more questions
- Ask for a verse and then a picture – practise this!

3.11 CREATIVITY – NON-VERBAL PRAYER

We pray to an incredibly creative God whose love and imagination designed the universe we live in and the people we love. In his creativity, God uses words, stories, dreams, pictures, music, creation, and so much more, to speak with and inspire his people. Why should we limit ourselves to only a few ways or means of talking back? Throughout church history, Christians have used art and music to focus on God and facilitate prayer and worship. Those who find silent or spoken prayer difficult can find a new language of communication in using symbols, art or actions to pray with others. When planning a prayer meeting, why not include different artistic mediums, activities and ways to engage the heart and focus the mind?

God gave us the ability to see, hear, touch, taste and smell. When planning times of prayer, why not engage all five of these senses:

WRITING ON THE WALL: PRAYER ROOM AT HTB

- **Sight:** Try using inspiring images, videos, text and bright colours to engage people visually in the things you are praying about. Why not pray in a location other than a church building? For example, you could chose an out door location with an inspiring view to help you pray for your area. You could also try creating a messy space to allow people to paint or draw their prayers for others to see and agree with.

- **Sound:** Think about how listening, speaking and singing could give people different experiences of prayer. Have music and instruments present. Psalm 100 talks about entering God's gates with thanksgiving and his courts with praise – musical worship can be an excellent catalyst to focused prayer.

- **Touch:** Fill the room with things to interact with. People who struggle with staying focused can find it helpful to sculpt their prayers, touch sand or water, or hold a cross or crown of thorns. Think about the different fabrics and textures you could use to shape the space. Also consider activities like lighting candles, writing in sand, blowing up balloons or lifting something to God that could help people pray.

- **Smell and taste:** You could burn incense and scented candles for an intimate atmosphere or you could use food in your prayer activities. Wine, bread, figs, honey and more are used as symbols throughout the Bible. Find ways to combine taste and prayer to help focus the mind and fellowship together.

Some people find it difficult to think creatively. Here's are a few questions to help you try:

What would you like people to pray about?

EXAMPLE ANSWER: Forgiveness from sin

What ideas, words or pictures do you associate with your answer?

EXAMPLE ANSWER: Sin = rubbish = between us and God = get rid of it = throw it away

What Bible verses can you find about it?

EXAMPLE ANSWER: Romans 6:6: 'For we know that our old self was crucified with him so that the body of sin might be done away with ...'

How could you shape your answers into an activity to focus the mind?

EXAMPLE ANSWER: Place a 'Bin for Sin' in front of a cross. Ask people to read Romans 6:6, then ask the Holy Spirit to reveal sin they need to confess. Provide pens and paper for people to write their sins on and throw them in the bin.

WHY NOT ENGAGE ALL FIVE OF THESE SENSES?

PRAYER GRAFFITI

49

4. PRAYER AND THE
ALPHA COURSE

'THE HARVEST IS PLENTIFUL BUT THE
WORKERS ARE FEW. ASK THE LORD OF
THE HARVEST, THEREFORE, TO SEND OUT
WORKERS INTO HIS HARVEST FIELD.'
//MATTHEW 9:37–38

PRAYER LIES AT THE HEART OF ANY ALPHA COURSE. WE WANT TO EMPOWER THE RE-EVANGELISATION OF THE NATIONS AND TRANSFORMATION OF SOCIETY BY CATALYSING, CONNECTING AND RESOURCING CHRIST-CENTRED, MISSION-MINDED PRAYER IN EVERY ALPHA CHURCH AROUND THE WORLD. IN THIS SECTION WE OUTLINE THREE SPECIFIC WAYS IN WHICH YOU CAN INCREASE THE PRAYER UNDERPINNING YOUR COURSE.

4.1 PRAYER FOR THE ALPHA INVITATION
4.2 PRAYER FOR ALPHA COURSE GUESTS
4.3 PRAYER WITH ALPHA COURSE GUESTS
4.4 PRAYER FOR ALPHA MISSION TRIPS(GAT)

4.1 PRAYER FOR THE ALPHA INVITATION

Every year a thrilling invitation goes out to the nation to come and explore the really big issues of life on an Alpha Course. Underpinning the national advertising campaign is an army of ordinary people, organising thousands of local Alpha Courses, booking venues, cooking meals, preparing to lead discussion groups, and inviting their friends.

But the story of the Alpha Invitation doesn't end there. Just as the real power behind the advertising campaign is the army of volunteers, so the real power

BEHIND THE SUCCESS OF THE ALPHA COURSE IS AN ARMY OF PRAYER WARRIORS WHO UNDERSTAND THAT THIS IS NOT JUST ABOUT MARKETING.

Behind the humorous talks and the pasta suppers is a real spiritual battle for hearts and minds.

Research in the UK revealed that there is an almost exact correlation between the amount of prayer mobilised for Alpha courses and the number of guests who attend the courses. As God says to King Zerubbabel,

'NOT BY MIGHT NOR BY POWER, BUT BY MY SPIRIT,' SAYS THE LORD ALMIGHTY' // ZECHARIAH 4:6.

So why not hold a prayer and worship event to launch your Alpha Course? Or maybe you could join with other churches in your local area to host a joint Alpha launch prayer event. Below is an example of an agenda we have found to be successful when running a sixty-minute Alpha Initiative prayer events along with some top tips to help your plan your event.

EXAMPLE AGENDA

Opening worship	10 minutes
Welcome and introduction	7 minutes
Testimony or interview slot	5 minutes
Prayer for Invitation and autumn Alpha courses	15 minutes
More worship	5 minutes
Prayer for the nation	5 minutes
Prayer for the church	10 minutes
Closing worship and prayer	3 minutes

TOP TIPS

- **Flexibility:** It is great to have a plan but don't feel that you have to rigidly stick to it. Allow time for the spirit to move. Some of the best prayer meetings we have had have been when things haven't gone entirely to plan!

- **Variety:** Use some of the prayer models suggested in section 3 of this guide to ensure that you keep people engaged. Everyone is different and people like to pray in different ways. Some like to pray out loud others like to pray in silence. Including a variety of prayer models will help to keep everyone involved.

THE ALPHA INVITATION

- **Testimonies:** Testimonies are a really important part of the evening. A great testimony of answered prayer is fantastic for building people's faith. Hearing a testimony from someone other than the church leader will encourage even the most sceptical of people to think, 'If their prayer can be answered then so can mine!' Also, hearing a great testimony from a person whose life has been transformed on the course is the best encouragement to pray for more lives to be transformed. People really connect with personal stories.

- **Worship:** Allow the worship to flow throughout the prayers. We have found that allowing the worship to continue quietly in the background while we pray sets the mood and keeps the meeting flowing.

A more detailed plan and resources to help you organise and run your prayer & worship launch event can be found at alpha.org/prayer

4.2 PRAYER FOR ALPHA COURSE GUESTS

The hosts and helpers, who facilitate the discussion groups on an Alpha Course, are best positioned to pray for the guests in their groups because they will come to know the names and needs of each individual in a way that no one else can. It is essential therefore that hosts and helpers really do pray regularly for their guests. There are at least three ways this can be done:

1. **Daily:** Aim to pray daily for the members of your group by name in your own personal devotional time. You may find it helpful to keep a list and make a few notes of anything the Lord shows you.

2. **Weekly:** The whole Alpha team should allow enough time to meet each week before the guests arrive for a briefing and prayer meeting. This is particularly important for the session 'Does God Heal Today?', as the team can wait on the Lord for words of knowledge, pictures and so on. These can then be read out after the talk and people who respond to them can be offered prayer.

3. **Occasionally:** It's a great idea for hosts and helpers to meet together occasionally apart from Alpha nights in order to pray for those in their small groups in an unhurried, less pressurised way.

While the hosts and helpers must take primary responsibility for praying for their guests, there may well be others in the church who would be willing to pray for the Alpha Course. Some churches therefore circulate prayer lists via email, and others have designed their own prayer bookmarks for the Alpha Course as a helpful reminder.

'WE WERE A SMALL TEAM, RUNNING ALPHA IN A SMALL RURAL CHURCH WITH ABOUT EIGHT GUESTS, ON AND OFF EACH WEEK! WE HAD TWO HOSTS AND TWO HELPERS AND A GREAT TASK FORCE. WE ALL MET UP BEFORE THE COURSE STARTED TO TRAIN AND PRAY FOR THE COURSE AND GUESTS. EACH WEEK WE PRAYED AHEAD OF THE SESSION. WE COULD NOT HAVE DONE IT WITHOUT PRAYER. THE LEADERS WERE ABLE TO MAKE IT EVERY WEEK, DESPITE MUCH NEED TO TRAVEL DURING THE COURSE. ALL THE TEAM WORKED TOGETHER WONDERFULLY AND WE HAD A REAL SENSE THAT GOD WAS CARRYING US ALL THROUGH.

ENCOURAGE TEAMS, HOWEVER SMALL, TO PRAY AND WAIT ON THE LORD FOR WORDS OR PICTURES AHEAD OF THE HEALING SESSION. WE DID JUST THIS AT THE PRAYERS BEFORE THE SESSION. ONE OF THE LEADERS HAD A WORD ABOUT AN EAR PROBLEM. WE LATER SHARED THAT WITH THE ALPHA GROUP, BUT NOTHING WAS SAID. AT THE END OF THE EVENING ONE OF THE HELPERS CAME UP AND SAID THAT SHE HAD BEEN SUFFERING WITH TINNITUS FOR YEARS BUT SAID NOTHING EARLIER AS SHE THOUGHT THE WORD COULD ONLY BE FOR ONE OF THE GUESTS! WHAT AN ENCOURAGEMENT IT WAS TO HER AND TO US ALL. IT BUILDS UP EXPECTATION AND FAITH FOR THE FUTURE TOO. WE WERE SO PLEASED THAT WE WAITED ON THE LORD FOR WHATEVER HE WISHED TO SAY TO US.'

REBECCA TAYLOR // WARWICKSHIRE, UK

4.3 PRAYER WITH ALPHA COURSE GUESTS

When you start praying with your small group will vary depending on who is in the group and how their journey is progressing. We recommend that you don't start praying as a small group until the session 'Why and How do I Pray?' This talk relates primarily to personal prayer, which is a good starting point as people come into relationship with God. Always remember that if you are not used to doing this, praying out loud can be extremely daunting. You may find that some groups are not ready to pray until after the sessions on the Holy Spirit. If possible try to pray together at least once prior to the talk 'Does God Heal Today?' This is so that if anyone responds to a word of knowledge about healing, it is less daunting for them to receive prayer.

Tips for praying together in the small group:

- Don't rush this! Be sensitive to where people are at spiritually – remember that praying out loud for the first time can be quite an intimidating experience
- Pray a short, simple prayer
- If you are going to open the session in prayer, say something like, 'I have asked John to open in prayer', so that the other guests will not be afraid that the leader might ask them to pray without giving notice at some time in the future

4.4 PRAYER FOR MISSION TRIPS (GAT)

Global Alpha Training is a type of mission trip, which was born at HTB and is quickly growing around the world; it is where global mission meets local evangelism. The aim of GAT is to enable people who know and love the Alpha Course to help train and equip others around the world to run the course. Teams of volunteers go from everywhere to anywhere.

In the last ten years, eighteen million have attended the Alpha Course. In a recent vision talk, Nicky Gumbel, the pioneer of the Alpha Course, shared his vision for that number to be increased to 100 million people in the next ten years. Global Alpha Training is integral to achieving that goal.

'THE HARVEST IS PLENTIFUL, BUT THE WORKERS ARE FEW. ASK THE LORD OF THE HARVEST, THEREFORE, TO SEND OUT WORKERS INTO HIS HARVEST FIELD.' // LUKE 10:1–2

Prayer and evangelisation go hand in hand. When you are going on a mission trip, whether that is a GAT trip or any other kind of mission, you are God's hands and feet going out and spreading the good news. It is therefore important to ensure that you, your team and the trip itself are adequately supported in prayer at every stage, from the planning right through to when you return.

Here then are some ways in which you can ensure your trip is covered in prayer:

1. **Pray regularly as a team:** Prayer is the most important thing you can do in preparing for an event. It ensures that at every stage you are keeping your focus on Jesus and brings you closer together as a team.

2. **Set up a prayer wheel:** Before you go, ask people to commit to praying for your event for one hour each day. Knowing that people are praying for you while you are away is a great comfort.

3. **Have one point of contact back home:** Instead of sending lots of emails to different people, designate one person as your point of contact who you can send prayer requests to. This person can then distribute them to everyone who is praying for you while you are away. This person could also send you any prophetic pictures of words of knowledge that people have had for the team.

4. **Pray morning and night during the trip:** It's a great idea, during your daily prayer meetings, to check how everyone is doing. You are going out to do amazing things but this can be very challenging and tiring. Issues, which may normally be small and easy to handle, may become magnified, so it's vital to pray.

5. **Share stories:** While you are away, you are going to hear all sorts of amazing stories and you'll see and hear encouraging answers to prayer. Share the stories! Hearing that their prayers have been answered will build the faith of everyone who has been praying for you while you have been away. It will also inspire others to step out of their comfort zone and go on a mission trip.

'WHAT A WONDERFUL EXPERIENCE THE PRISON VISIT WAS. WE THOUGHT WE MIGHT JUST SEE A FEW INMATES WHO WERE DOING THE ALPHA COURSE. WE WERE ESCORTED INTO THE PRISON COURTYARD WHERE 1052 INMATES WERE READY AND WAITING, WANTING TO HEAR ABOUT ALPHA, TO RECEIVE SOME VERSES FROM THE BIBLE AND SOME PRAYERS OF HOPE INTO THEIR LIVES. AT THE END WHEN WE SAID THE 'SORRY, THANK YOU, PLEASE' PRAYER, JUST IN CASE ONE PERSON WANTED TO GIVE THEIR LIFE TO CHRIST, WE ASKED, 'HOW MANY PEOPLE RESPONDED TO THAT PRAYER?' AND 80 PER CENT OF THE INMATES PUT UP THEIR HANDS. WOW! WHAT AN EMOTIONAL EXPERIENCE THIS WAS. WE DID NOT TAKE JESUS INTO THE PRISON; HE WAS ALREADY THERE – BIG TIME!'

5. PRAYER RESOURCES

'LORD, TEACH US TO PRAY.'
// LUKE 11:1

RECOMMENDED BOOKS

VISION FOR PRAYER

The Art of Prayer: A Simple Guide to Conversation with God by Timothy Jones (Waterbook Press, 2005)
A simple, practical and engaging introduction to different types of prayer.

Red Moon Rising: The Adventure of Faith & The Power of Prayer by Pete Greig and Dave Roberts (Kingsway, 2003)
The amazing story of the rise of the 24-7 Prayer movement – a real faith-builder and great for all ages.

Prayer: Finding the Heart's True Home by Richard Foster (HarperCollins, 1996)
Hailed by many as the most important contemporary book on Christian prayer.

The Message of Prayer by Tim Chester (IVP, 2003)
A solid, biblical survey of the biblical teaching on prayer, ideal for leaders.

Prayer: Does it Make Any Difference? By Philip Yancey (Hodder, 2006)
A great overview of prayer, particularly for those asking questions about how it works.

STORIES OF ANSWERED PRAYER

Mountain Rain: A Biography of James O. Fraser, Pioneer Missionary to China by Eileen Crossman (OMF, 1994)
An inspiring account of a pioneer missionary and an enduring testament to the power of prayer in mission.

The Autobiography of George Müller by George Müller and Diana L. Matisko (Whitaker House, 1984)
One of the most remarkable modern stories of God's miraculous provision in answer to believing prayer.

Healed of Cancer by Dodie Osteen (Struik Christian Books, 1987)

MODELS OF PRAYER

Prayer Walking by Steve Hawthorne and Graham Kendrick (Charisma Media, 1993)

Becoming the Answer to our Prayers: Prayer for Ordinary Radicals by Shane Claiborne and Johnathon Wilson-Hartgrove (IVP Books, 2008)
Shane Claiborne and Jonathan Wilson-Hartgrove show how prayer and action must go together.

Intercessory Prayer by Dutch Sheets (Regal, 1997)
A simple, inspiring introduction to intercessory prayer. Great for beginners.

The Sword of the Spirit, The Word of God by Joy Lamb (Lamb Books, Inc. 1993)
Praying God's word for the healing of our land.

The 24-7 Prayer Manual (David C. Cook 2010)
A practical guide book to help you set up a successful season of 24-7 Prayer in your church, with fascinating historical and motivational sections.

HEALING THROUGH PRAYER

Surprised by the Power of the Spirit by Jack Deere (Zondervan, 2010)
This book presents both personal and biblical reasons why God still speaks and heals today

HEARING GOD'S VOICE

Listening to God: Hearing His Voice by Joyce Huggett (Hodder & Stoughton, 2005)
Practical guidance and advice for anyone seeking a new dimension of prayer.

Surprised by the Voice of God by Jack Deere (Zondervan, 1998)
Takes you to the Bible to discover the variety of creative, deeply personal ways God still communicates with us today.

Inspirations from a Paper Boat by Virginia Duhanes (Leprosy Mission International, 2001)
Each short chapter in this book will not only encourage and uplift you, but also challenge you to be still and listen for God's voice in your own life. Perfect reading for a daily quiet time.

More by Simon Ponsonby (Cook, 2010)
The author seeks to deal with the constant struggle that we have as Christians to understand how we can know more of God.

God on Mute by Pete Greig (Kingsway 2007)
Written out of Pete Greig's own experience of the miraculous power of prayer alongside the pain of unanswered prayer and the common human struggle to find faith with that paradox.

STORIES OF CHANGED LIVES

Life Change: Fifteen men tell their extrodinary story edited by Mark Elsdon-Dew (Alpha International, 2011)

RECOMMENDED ONLINE RESOURCES

24-7Prayer.com

revivalrun.org

gat.alpha.org

htb.org.uk/prayer

The Lord's Prayer Teaching Series from HTB by Pete Greig: A nine part journey through the 'Our Father' exploring different aspects and approaches to prayer. Available from: htb.org.uk/media

Bible in One Year with Nicky Gumbel: htb.org.uk/bible-in-one-year

RESOURCES CURRENTLY UNDER DEVELOPMENT

The Prayer Course
A 6 to 12 week journey for small groups going deeper in prayer. For more information email prayer@htb.org.uk